LET'S GO ON AN ADVENTURE!

Written and Illustrated by

Annesley Williams

♥

"Keep reading. It's one of the most
marvelous adventures that
anyone can have."
-Lloyd Alexander

LET'S GO ON AN ADVENTURE!

ISBN-13: 978-1484 056318
ISBN-10: 1484056310

Thank you to everyone who bought this book!
Your support and encouragement means the world to me.
I love you all.

♥

To see more of my work visit
www.facebook.com/annesleyart & annesleywilliams.tumblr.com

Special thanks to Kait and Scarlet Payne
for sharing your beautiful story
and being the inspiration for this book.
May you both continue to see everyday as an adventure.

This book is dedicated to my mom,
who instilled such a sense of wonder
and a love for adventure in me at such an early age.
You will always be my #1 adventure buddy.

LET'S GO ON AN ADVENTURE!

Written and Illustrated by

Annesley Williams

Let's go on an adventure
and sail to far away lands.
We will go fishing for goldfish
and make castles on the sand.

Let's go on an adventure
to catch a million fireflies.
We will pretend we just caught
all the stars in the sky.

Let's go on an adventure
on a tightrope so high.
We wont ever fall,
we will touch the sky.

Let's go on an adventure
and dance till the sun goes down.
We won't have a care in the world,
just me and you and our dancing shoes.

Let's go on an adventure,
and fly into outer space.
We can go to another planet or float
around the moon with grace.

Let's go on an adventure
to a place where we are kings
and queens. We will march around,
and we will own the scene.

Let's go on an adventure.
So much to do and so much to see.
There's always adventure,
as long as there's you,
and as long as there's me.